Michelle's MVP Award

A Chemical Engineering Story

Written by the Engineering is Elementary Team

Illustrated by Keith Favazza

Chapter One | An MVP Award

"Hi, Tim," Michelle greeted her older brother as he walked into the kitchen. He set down his hockey gear and smiled.

"Hey, Michelle," Tim said. "Ready for practice?"

"Almost ready," she said. "I have to make a maple leaf."

Michelle grabbed the bag of play dough she'd made earlier. She made a play dough maple leaf before every hockey practice. The maple leaf was the name and symbol for the school team Michelle and Tim played on—just like the professional hockey team, the Toronto Maple Leafs. After every practice, Michelle let Coach Boucher give her maple leaf to the most valuable player—the MVP.

"Who do you think Coach Boucher will give your MVP

award to today?" Tim asked, as Michelle flattened the dough.

"I bet you'll get it," Michelle said. "You're the best player on the team!"

"Thanks," Tim said. "But I bet Coach Boucher will give you the award today. You've been playing really well."

"I'm getting better," Michelle said. "Some of the kids still think I can't play. Jason thinks I'm bad."

"Why would you say that?" asked Tim. "I bet he thinks you're doing a great job."

Michelle shook her head no. Michelle and Jason were in the same class. Sometimes when she had trouble reading, she thought Jason looked at her funny.

Michelle had been born with Down Syndrome. Usually being different didn't bother Michelle. Mom and Dad always told her that everyone is different. That's what makes every person special. Michelle didn't mind asking for help with things like reading or hockey. Once in a while, though, she wished she didn't feel quite so different.

At least I never need help with art, Michelle thought. *I am good at making play dough and cutting out shapes.* She looked at the cookie cutters on the counter and thought about how proud she felt the first time she made a maple leaf for her team. Now she could make all kinds of animals and plants. Michelle noticed Tim watching her cut out the leaf.

"Do you want to try?" she asked.

Tim looked at the dough and the cookie cutters in front of him. "I guess so," he said. "But I don't know what to do."

"It's easy," Michelle said. She held up her leaf for him to see and then put it in a plastic bowl so she could carry it to practice. Tim grabbed some of the dough and rolled it between his hands.

"Why do you do this before every practice?" Tim asked. "Don't you get tired of it?"

"No," Michelle said. "Everyone who does something good for the team should get a reward."

"Maybe we could ask Coach Boucher to change the team name so you could make something else," Tim said. Tim looked down at the lumpy glob of dough he was trying to cut. "Do you think our team name could be changed to the . . . Blobs?" he asked. They both giggled.

"After hockey practice I'm going to make something special out of play dough," Michelle said. "Something for Uncle Adam. I'll show you how to do it."

Uncle Adam was their mom's brother. He lived in Montreal, but he was visiting Michelle's family for a few weeks. Michelle wanted to make him a play dough present before he left.

"Hey, guys!" Mom called from the next room. "Let's get your stuff together and head out to the rink." Tim and Michelle pulled on their thick winter coats and followed Mom out the door.

A Special Announcement

Michelle loved to be on the ice with her team. She tried hard to play well and practice the passes that Tim had shown her. But by the end of practice, Michelle was tired.

"Let's try one last shot," Tim called from across the ice.

Michelle swung her hockey stick back and hit the puck. It skidded off, but not where she'd wanted it to go. Michelle watched as Jason swooped in, stopped the puck, and skated off with it. *Now Jason must really think I'm bad*, she thought. Just then, the buzzer sounded, signaling the end of practice. Everyone skated toward the bench.

"I didn't do a good job today," Michelle said to Tim as he pulled off his helmet.

Tim patted her on the shoulder. "Nah, you did great."

Coach waved his hand and motioned for the team to gather round. "Nice job, everyone," he said.

"Almost everyone," muttered Jason. Michelle wondered if Jason was talking about her. Even though Tim said she'd done well, she still felt like she let the team down.

"Today's MVP maple leaf goes to . . . Tim! You were a real team player today." The whole team clapped. Michelle clapped extra hard. "Before you all head out, I have a special announcement," Coach continued. Michelle paused as she was unlacing her skate. She looked up at him. "One of my hockey teammates from college has just started working for the Toronto Maple Leafs."

"The Maple Leafs?" cried Tim. "Wow! Maybe he'll get to meet Mats Sundin." Mats Sundin was the captain for the Maple Leafs.

"Guess what?" Coach said. "We might *all* get to meet Mats Sundin!"

The whole team started to cheer. Michelle's mouth fell open as she looked at Tim. Tim had all of Mats's posters and his jersey.

"Okay, listen up." Coach Boucher called them all to order. "My friend said that if we can get tickets to next month's game at the Air Canada Center, he'll set up a special meeting with Mats Sundin after the game. You all know the school's annual fundraising fair is coming up. This year, we need to think of something extra special to do at the fair, so we can raise enough money for those tickets. Tomorrow, let's meet to think about possibilities. See you then!"

Chapter Three | A Play Dough Plan

The next day, Michelle and Tim walked into the locker room where the team was meeting before practice. They sat down on one of the benches. Michelle set the plastic container holding the day's MVP maple leaf on her lap.

"All right, everyone," called Coach Boucher, his voice echoing through the room. "Raise your hand if you want to see the Maple Leafs play!"

Michelle threw her hand into the air. All of her teammates were waving their arms, too. Coach Boucher smiled and clapped his big hands together.

"Great!" he said. "I figured out that we need to raise three hundred dollars to buy enough tickets for all of us to see the game."

"Three hundred dollars?!" Tim cried.

"I know that sounds like a lot," continued Coach Boucher, "but you're a determined team if I've ever seen one. How do you think we can raise the money?"

The room was quiet. *Money,* Michelle thought. *How can we raise money?*

"A bake sale could work," Mike said.

"The baseball team does that every year," said Jason. "That's not cool enough."

"The art club sold paintings at the fair last year," said Beth. "That was different."

"But we need to do something really special," said Jason. "We need to make everyone at the fair want to come to our booth."

"Hey!" Tim cried. "I know what we can do!" Everyone in the room turned around to face him. Michelle saw that Tim was staring at the container she held. The maple leaf she'd made showed through the plastic. "Can I hold up your maple leaf?" Tim asked.

"Sure," Michelle said. She wondered what Tim had figured out.

Tim set the maple leaf in the palm of his hand. Then he held it up for everyone to see. "We could have a booth where people make stuff out of play dough. Just like Michelle

does. We could make all kinds of shapes, even animals and plants."

"Yeah," Andrew said. "We could cut out stars and trees and even tigers."

Coach Boucher nodded. "I really like this idea. Michelle, you're the one who knows a lot about sculpting. What do you think?"

Michelle felt her heart beating fast. She looked around at her teammates and then at Coach Boucher. "Making the dough is the fun part," Michelle said. "Can we teach people how to do that, too?"

"Michelle's right," said Tim. "We should let people make the dough. If we write down the directions, everyone could do it."

"What do you think, team?" asked Coach Boucher. Michelle looked around the room and saw the team nodding. Jason was staring down at the floor. *Is he mad?* Michelle wondered. Finally she looked back to see what Coach had to say.

"I agree—this is a great idea!" he said. "Michelle, do you think you and Tim can come up with a plan for how we can do this?"

Michelle nodded, even though her mouth felt dry and her palms were sweaty. No one outside of her family ever asked Michelle to do really important things.

"Okay then, let's get on the ice. Next week, when we meet again, we'll find out what Michelle and Tim have figured out," said Coach.

Tim and me, Michelle thought. *I always have to get help from Tim. But I'm good at art all by myself.*

Before Michelle could think about working on her own

anymore, she noticed Jason talking to Tim.

"Following directions to make play dough?" Jason asked. "No one's going to want to read directions. That's not fun."

"I've done it before," said Tim. "It *is* fun. You'll see."

"Well, you better help her," Jason said. "The team really needs this money."

He's right, Michelle thought. *I need to do a great job. But I want to do this on my own.*

Chapter Four | Help From Uncle Adam

After practice, Michelle and Tim saw Mom's big green station wagon in front of the school. Michelle grabbed her bag and ran to the car. She could hear Tim's bag bumping against his side as he jogged behind her. As she got closer to the car, she could see it wasn't Mom who was there to pick them up.

"Uncle Adam!" Michelle cried, sliding into the backseat. "Guess what? We're going to see Mats Sundin!"

"No kidding!" said Uncle Adam. "How did you manage that?" Michelle and Tim explained what Coach Boucher had told them, and the plan they'd come up with to raise money for the team.

"That's great," Uncle Adam said. "Michelle, you're

always showing me ways to make even complicated things easy. I'm sure you can show everyone on your team what to do."

"My dough never comes out as well as Michelle's," Tim said. "I'm just not good at art stuff."

"Don't say that," Michelle said. "You can be good at it. There are lots of steps you have to do. You have to follow the recipe, then make the shapes."

"This whole thing sounds like a great project," said Uncle Adam. "It reminds me of what I do for my work. Sometimes in my job I use steps and directions that are a lot like recipes. We just have a different name for them—we call them processes."

"What's the difference?" asked Tim.

"Good question!" said Uncle Adam. "Usually when people use the word recipe, they're talking about all the steps and ingredients you need to make some type of food. A process can be the materials and the directions needed to make all kinds of different things."

"Things like my play dough maple leaves?" asked Michelle.

"Sure," said Uncle Adam. "I design lots of different processes for my job. Did you two know I'm a chemical engineer?"

"What's that?" asked Michelle.

"Is it like being a scientist?" asked Tim. "Do you wear a white lab coat and work with stuff in test tubes?"

"Sometimes I do work with test tubes," said Uncle Adam, "but I'm not a scientist. Chemical engineers use what we know about chemistry and math, plus some creativity, to solve problems and create new things. I've worked on lots of cool problems in my job—like helping design perfumes that smell a certain way, and designing ways to make better paint for artists."

"Paint?" Michelle asked. "I use paint in my art all the time! I'm sure you can help me with the play dough."

"I have an idea," said Uncle Adam. "How about if the three of us work on this play dough process project when we get home?"

Michelle was quiet. She shook her head no and looked over at Tim. "I want to do this myself," she said. "Uncle Adam can help me. Then I can show the team all by myself."

Tim held up his hand and gave Michelle a high five. "That's a good idea," said Tim. "I know you can do it. I can't wait to see what you come up with."

| Chapter Five | # A Work in Progress |

Michelle and Uncle Adam sat down at the kitchen table.

"Okay, let's get started," said Uncle Adam. "Maybe I should tell you about one of the ways I figure out how to design things at work. You might like to use it, too. It's called the engineering design process."

"What's that?" asked Michelle.

"It's a set of steps that helps me solve all kinds of problems," said Uncle Adam. "I bet you've already started it. How did you first learn how to make your play dough?"

"Dad helped me. We found recipes on the Internet," said Michelle. "We tried three of them. Some didn't work. I'll show you." She walked over to the cabinet and pulled out an old piece of paper dotted with water spots. There were pencil marks where Michelle's dad had helped her write down the changes they'd made to the recipe.

"We had to add less liquid—less water," said Michelle. She'd been learning about the differences between liquids and solids in school. "When there was too much water, the dough was mushy," she explained. "The flour and the salt are solids. They don't make the play dough mushy, but if you add them in the wrong order, the dough is bad."

"Yep, just as I thought," said Uncle Adam. "You're an engineer, just like me! You've already started the engineering design process. You've asked questions about how to make good play dough. And you've investigated how other people made it. We're starting the next step of the

engineering design process right now: imagining. We need to imagine different ways to explain the play dough process to your team. Do you think we should show the team these directions?" he asked, pointing to the paper.

Michelle thought for a few moments. "Those directions are hard," she said. "We should think of better ways to explain the steps. Can we draw pictures, too?"

"That's a great idea!" said Uncle Adam. "You can show the process to your team using words and pictures."

"I'll draw," Michelle said. "Can you write the steps?"

"Sure can," said Uncle Adam. "Drawing and writing will help us with the next steps of the engineering design process. We'll plan the process and then create play dough."

Uncle Adam helped Michelle gather everything they

needed to make the dough. After Michelle showed him each step of the process, he wrote down what she had done. On a different paper, Michelle drew a picture of the step.

"Let's see," Uncle Adam said, after they'd been working for a while. "We have steps for measuring the ingredients and mixing the dough."

"And for cutting out the shapes!" Michelle said, clapping her hands together. "We're all done!"

"Well, we're almost done," Uncle Adam said. "We made the leaves, but our goal is to design the process so other people can make them, too, right?"

"Right," said Michelle. "The process needs to be good enough for anyone to use."

"The last step of the engineering design process helps you make sure your design is the best it can be," said Uncle Adam.

"That's what I need," said Michelle. "What's the last step?"

"It's improving what we did. Let's ask Tim to try out the process we designed. Then we can try to make it even better."

Chapter Six | Is It Magic?

Michelle called Tim into the kitchen. She and Uncle Adam showed him one page with written directions and another with pictures of the steps of the process.

"I think I've got it," said Tim. "Can I try it out?"

"Yeah!" said Michelle. "I can't wait to see if our process works."

"Michelle, you and I shouldn't say anything," said Uncle Adam. "We really need to test the process we designed. We'll just watch what Tim does. At the end we can talk about how well it worked."

Tim measured out the water, the salt, and the flour and dumped it all into a bowl. Then he started to mix everything together.

Michelle clapped her hand over her mouth. *That's not how it should be!* she thought.

"Um, I don't think I did this right," said Tim, as he picked up a lump of grainy, gooey play dough.

Uncle Adam laughed. Michelle felt like she was about to burst! "It's okay, Michelle," Uncle Adam said. "Tell him what's wrong."

"We need to explain the order of the steps!" she cried. "You can't mix everything together all at once. You need to mix just the first two ingredients to start. Then you add the last one later."

"Okay, I'll try that," said Tim. He started over again. When Tim didn't understand what to do, they all worked together to think of a better way to explain it. After following the whole process, Tim held up a maple leaf.

"Look, Michelle," Tim said. "No more blobs!"

"I'm glad the process works," said Michelle. "But what if the other kids think this is too hard?" she asked.

"They won't," said Tim. "If they follow all the steps, they'll be able to make something really cool."

"Think about what you told me earlier, Michelle," Uncle Adam said. "You use liquids and solids to make this play dough: water, salt, and flour. When you do the process the right way, you end up with a dough that isn't like the water or the salt or the flour. It's soft and squishy and you can make shapes out of it."

"Yeah," said Tim. "It's almost like magic!"

"It's better than magic," said Uncle Adam. "It's chemical engineering! And the process that Michelle created is a technology."

"Technology?" asked Michelle.

"Yep," said Uncle Adam. "Technology is any thing or process that helps you solve a problem. This process helps you explain to your team how to make play dough sculptures."

Michelle smiled. "So I designed a process and a technology for my team," she said. "I hope they like it. Uncle Adam, will you come with us to show the team?"

"I wouldn't miss it for the world," Uncle Adam answered.

Chapter Seven | Testing With the Team

On the day of their next practice, Michelle, Tim, and Uncle Adam carried shopping bags of salt, flour, measuring cups, and plastic bowls into the school auditorium. Michelle handed Coach Boucher a stack of papers. Each one had "Play Dough Process" written across the top. Uncle Adam and Tim helped Michelle set up the materials. Then Coach called everyone together.

"Let's read these directions," Coach said. "Then we can all start to mix up the ingredients that Michelle and Tim brought."

Michelle looked out into the auditorium. She could see everyone reading the papers on the table in front of them. Everyone except Jason.

One by one, the teammates started to come up to the table. Michelle showed Beth how to measure out the flour so that the cup was filled to the very top, and which line the water should reach. When Michelle handed Beth a mixing bowl to combine everything, she noticed Coach Boucher leaning over Jason's seat. Jason had his arms crossed, and he was scowling and looking down at the floor.

"I don't want to read the directions. This is stupid," Michelle heard him say. "It's never going to work."

"Let's give it a try," urged Coach Boucher. "We'll do it together."

Michelle watched as Coach Boucher walked towards her. Jason followed a few steps behind him, dragging his feet and holding the paper directions.

"Michelle, can you explain this process to Jason and me?" Coach asked.

Jason set the directions down on the table. Michelle flipped to the second page where she had drawn pictures of the steps. Then she took a deep breath and started explaining. "We need to measure out two scoops of flour," she said, pointing down at the pictures.

"Wait," Jason said. "I didn't notice those. The pictures tell me the same things as the words?"

"Yeah," Michelle said. Jason kept looking down at the

pictures, so she added, "Sometimes it's hard for me to read directions. I like the pictures better."

"Yeah," Jason said slowly. "Me, too. So it looks like next you need to measure one scoop of water."

"Right!" Michelle said.

Jason and Michelle went through the whole process together. When they were done, Jason held up a great maple leaf to show Coach Boucher.

"That's great, guys!" Coach Boucher said. "Tim and Michelle, you should be proud of this play dough process."

"I didn't do anything," said Tim. "It was all Michelle!"

"I stand corrected," Coach Boucher said. "Michelle, you really came through for the team."

"Thanks," said Michelle. "I'm excited! I'm sure we'll get to see the Maple Leafs!"

A few weeks later, Michelle, Tim, and the rest of the team sat in the stands of the Air Canada Center. Michelle was on the edge of her seat. She couldn't wait to see the real Toronto Maple Leafs play! A voice boomed from the speakers above their heads, announcing all of the players.

"Number 13, Mats Sundin!" said the announcer. The whole team stood up and clapped. Michelle saw Tim jumping up and down.

"Hey, Michelle," called Jason. "I have something for you." Jason held up a play dough maple leaf, twice as big as the ones Michelle usually made.

"The whole team made this," Jason explained. "Today you're the most valuable player!"

Michelle smiled. Not only had she done something good for the team all by herself, but she had made a new friend in the process.

TORONTO
MAPLE
LEAFS

Try It!

A Play Dough Process

Have you ever made play dough? In the story, Michelle lists the ingredients you need: flour, salt, and water. Using those ingredients and thinking about a sculpture that you would like to make, your goal is to create a play dough process. Once you've finished, you can make sculptures, just like Michelle and her team did!

Materials
- [ ] 2 scoops of flour
- [ ] 1 scoop of salt
- [ ] 1 scoop of warm water
- [ ] Bowl
- [ ] Measuring scoop
- [ ] Spoon
- [ ] Toothpicks
- [ ] Paint
- [ ] Paint brush

Asking About Play Dough

Combining 2 scoops of flour, 1 scoop of salt, and 1 scoop of water will make a play dough that's good for sculpting. But the order in which you combine the ingredients is important. What happens if you mix the water and the flour first? What about when you dump everything into a bowl and mix it all together at once? How about mixing the salt and the water first, and then adding the flour? Which process makes the best play dough?

Imagine and Plan a Sculpture

What are you going to sculpt? You might want to make an animal or a plant. What are the shapes making up the object you want to sculpt? Are there circles, squares, or triangles? Can you draw a picture of your object using those shapes? In what order should you put the shapes together to make your sculpture?

Create!

Try making your sculpture. You might want to make each shape separately. You can poke toothpicks into the shapes to help join them together. You can paint your sculpture after it dries. Did you follow the plan that you came up with? What worked well? What didn't? Write down your play dough sculpture-making process using words, or draw it out with pictures. Try giving your process to a friend to see if he or she can make play dough and create a sculpture.

Improve Your Process

Use the engineering design process to improve your play dough process. Ask your friend which parts of your process worked well and which parts did not. Once you've improved it, you and your friend can try the process together.

See What Others Have Done

See what other kids have done at http://www.mos.org/eie/tryit. What did you try? You can submit your solutions and pictures to our website, and maybe we'll post your submission!

Glossary

Chemical Engineer: Someone who combines his or her knowledge of math and science, especially chemistry, to design technologies and solve problems.

Down Syndrome: A disorder caused by a genetic abnormality with several symptoms, including learning disabilities and specific body characteristics.

Engineer: A person who uses his or her creativity and knowledge of mathematics and science to design things or processes that solve problems.

Engineering Design Process: The steps that engineers use to design something to solve a problem.

Liquid: A state of matter in which the substance is fluid and takes the shape of its container, like water in a glass.

Process: A series of steps to meet a goal.

Sculpt: To shape or design a work of art.

Solid: A state of matter in which the substance is not fluid and holds its shape, such as water in the form of ice.

Technology: Any thing or process that people create and use to solve a problem.